FOR EVERYONE WHO,
LIKE MYSELF,
HAS EVER FELT
A LITTLE DIFFERENT

Henry Holt and Company, LLC
PUBLISHERS SINCE 1866
175 Fifth Avenue
New York, New York 10010
mackids.com

Henry Holt® is a registered trademark of
Henry Holt and Company, LLC.
Copyright © 2013 by David Milgrim
All rights reserved.

Library of Congress Cataloging-in-Publication Data
Milgrim, David.
Some monsters are different / David Milgrim. — 1st ed.
p.   cm.
Summary: Monsters celebrate their individuality.
ISBN 978-0-8050-9519-7 (hardcover)
[1. Individuality–Fiction. 2. Monsters–Fiction.] I. Title.
PZ7.M5955So 2013   [E]–dc23   2012016355

First Edition—2013
The artist used digital ink and pastel to create the
illustrations for this book.
Printed in China by Macmillan Production Asia Ltd.,
Kowloon Bay, Hong Kong (vendor code 10)

10 9 8 7 6 5 4 3 2 1

SOME MONSTERS ARE DIFFERENT

DAVID MILGRIM

HENRY HOLT AND COMPANY • NEW YORK

SOME

MONSTERS ARE AFRAID.

SOME ARE NOT.

SOME MONSTERS WILL EAT ANYTHING.

SOME ARE PICKY.

SOME MONSTERS TALK AND TALK AND TALK.

SOME ARE QUIET.

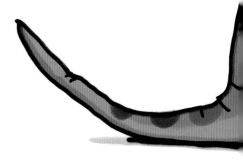

SOME MONSTERS ARE
ALIKE.

SOME MONSTERS ARE DIFFERENT.

SOME MONSTERS
LOVE TO DANCE.

SOME LIKE TO WATCH.

SOME
MONSTERS LOVE TO
PLAY OUTSIDE.

SOME LIKE IT INSIDE.

SOME
MONSTERS DON'T MAKE
ANY FUSS AT ALL WHEN
THEY HAVE TO TAKE
A BATH.

SOME DO.

BUT...

ALL
MONSTERS ARE
ABSOLUTELY, POSITIVELY,
COMPLETELY, PERFECTLY
WONDERFUL...

JUST THE WAY
THEY ARE!